I dedicate my first book to the love of my life, my wife, Jennifer,
and our four little miracles: Mitchell, Patrick, Jessica, and Jeffrey
—A.K.

To Pearl Annie Teghtmeyer Lammle, with love
—L.L.

Pajama Pirates

Text copyright © 2010 by Andrew Kramer

Illustrations copyright © 2010 by Leslie Lammle

Manufactured in China.

Library of Congress Cataloging-in-Publication Data is available.

ISBN 978-0-06-125194-8 (trade bdg.) — ISBN 978-0-06-125195-5 (lib. bdg.)

Typography by Rachel Zegar

Title design by Iskra Johnson

10 11 12 13 14 SCP 10 9 8 7 6 5 4 3 2 1

❖

First Edition

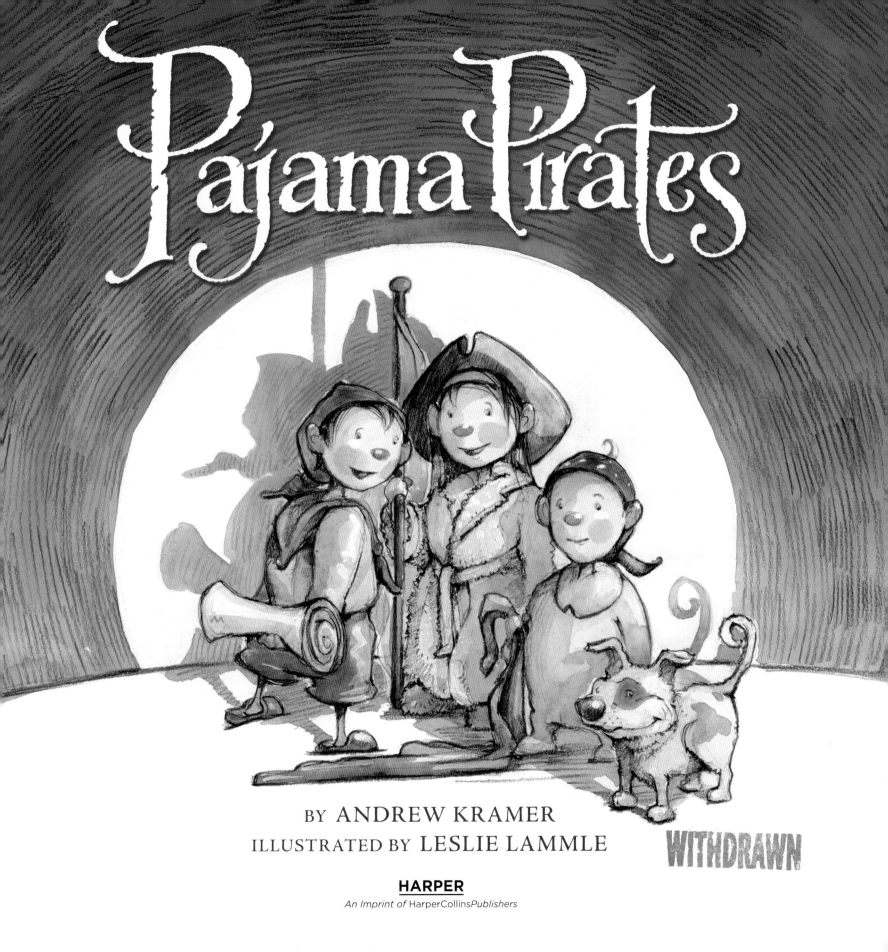

Pajama Pirates

BY ANDREW KRAMER

ILLUSTRATED BY LESLIE LAMMLE

HARPER

An Imprint of HarperCollinsPublishers

The moon begins
its evening show.

Pajama pirates yell,
"Oh no!"

Let others sleep;
their day is done.
The treasure hunt
has just begun.

To the ship they start to row.
Pajama pirates on the go.
A moonlit path leads from the bay.

A stolen map to chart the way.
But in the dark, another ship!
Pirate grins begin to slip.

start here

The flag reveals not friend but foe.
Pajama pirates on the go.

It's too late! The ship draws near.
Pajama pirates show no fear.

A clash of swords. A bitter fight.
Then more pirates come in sight.
Up the sides more pirates climb.

A plan, a plan . . .
they're out of time!
Then through the fog,
a cannon blast rips the sail
and splits the mast.

"Ye be shark bait, swim or sink!"
Pajama pirates stop to think.

Rival ships from coast to coast.
Pajama pirates make a ghost.

Other ships don't know it's fake.
Pirate knees begin to quake.

Pajama pirates raise swords high.
Lightning splits across the sky.

The other pirates know they're beat.
And soon begin a fast retreat.
The battle's won. The coast is clear.
Pajama pirates shout and cheer.

But . . . clouds roll in, a sudden squall.
It's Mama Nature's final call.
"Climb the rigging. Trim the sail!
Hoist the anchor. Hold the rail.
Batten hatches, spin the wheel."

"Just five more minutes, please?"

"No deal."

The crew surrenders tired oars
and lands the ship on sandy shores.

They walk the plank
now, one by one.
"G'night mateys . . .
sure was fun."

A sweet wind blows;
they're tucked in tight.
With pirate dreams
to fill the night.
Of buried treasure,
found at last.
To buy new oars
and fix the mast.
Thread for sails
they'll need to sew.

Pajama pirates on the go.